THE CRETACEOUS CHASE

DINOSAUR COVE

DINOSAUR COVE™

THE CRETACEOUS CHASE

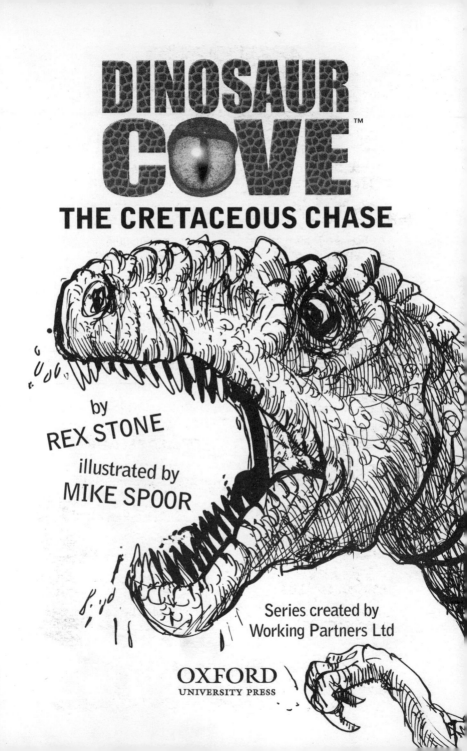

by
REX STONE

illustrated by
MIKE SPOOR

Series created by
Working Partners Ltd

OXFORD
UNIVERSITY PRESS

Special thanks to Jane Clarke

For Alex Dingwall, age 7, who loves Dinosaur Cove!

For Angel Browne, Kathy, Cathy, Book Week members, staff, and all the students at the Anglo American School, Sofia, Bulgaria—with thanks for making my illustration workshop visit such a wonderful experience   M.S.

OXFORD
UNIVERSITY PRESS

Great Clarendon Street, Oxford OX2 6DP
Oxford University Press is a department of the University of Oxford.
It furthers the University's objective of excellence in research, scholarship,
and education by publishing worldwide in

Oxford   New York

Auckland   Cape Town   Dar es Salaam   Hong Kong   Karachi
Kuala Lumpur   Madrid   Melbourne   Mexico City   Nairobi
New Delhi   Shanghai   Taipei   Toronto

With offices in

Argentina   Austria   Brazil   Chile   Czech Republic   France   Greece
Guatemala   Hungary   Italy   Japan   Poland   Portugal   Singapore
South Korea   Switzerland   Thailand   Turkey   Ukraine   Vietnam

Oxford is a registered trade mark of Oxford University Press
in the UK and in certain other countries

British Library Cataloguing in Publication Data

Data available

ISBN: 978-0-19-275627-5

1 3 5 7 9 10 8 6 4 2

Printed in Great Britain
Paper used in the production of this book is a natural,
recyclable product made from wood grown in sustainable forests
The manufacturing process conforms to the environmental
regulations of the country of origin

FACT FILE

▷ JAMIE AND HIS BEST FRIEND, TOM, HAVE
AN AMAZING SECRET. THEY KNOW THE WAY TO DINOSAUR
WORLD! NO ONE EXCEPT THE BOYS HAS EVER BEEN
THERE—UNTIL NACHO THE PUPPY FOLLOWS THEM INTO
THE CRETACEOUS. AT FIRST THE BOYS THINK IT'S GREAT
FUN HAVING A PUPPY WITH THEM, AND NACHO EVEN
PLAYS WITH WANNA, THE BOYS' DINO FRIEND. BUT THE
MOOD CHANGES WHEN NACHO DISAPPEARS. WILL THE
BOYS FIND HIM BEFORE HE BUMPS INTO THE TERRIFYING
ALBERTOSAURUS?

JAMIE

- FULL NAME: JAMIE MORGAN
- AGE: 8 YEARS
- SIZE: 1 JATOM*
- TOP SPEED: 10 KPH
- LIKES: FOSSIL HUNTING AND
LEARNING ABOUT DINOSAURS
- DISLIKES: BEING STUCK
INDOORS

Jamie's eye

Jamie's foot

Jamie's hand

*NOTE A JATOM IS THE SIZE OF JAMIE OR TOM: 125 CM TALL AND 27 KG IN WEIGHT

TOM

- FULL NAME: THOMAS CLAY
- AGE: 8 YEARS
- SIZE: 1 JATOM*
- TOP SPEED: 10 KPH
- LIKES: TRACKING ANIMALS AND EXPLORING WILDLIFE
- DISLIKES: RAINY DAYS

Tom's eye

Tom's hand

WANNA

- FULL NAME: WANNANOSAURUS
- AGE: 65–80 MILLION YEARS**
- SIZE: LESS THAN A JATOM*
- TOP SPEED: 50 KPH, ESPECIALLY WHEN BEING CHASED BY A T-REX
- LIKES: STINKY GINGKO FRUIT AND BANGING HIS HEAD ON TREE TRUNKS
- DISLIKES: SCARY DINOSAURS

Wanna's head

Wanna's foot

*NOTE: A JATOM IS THE SIZE OF JAMIE OR TOM: 125 CM TALL AND 27 KG IN WEIGHT
**NOTE: SCIENTISTS CALL THIS PERIOD THE LATE CRETACEOUS

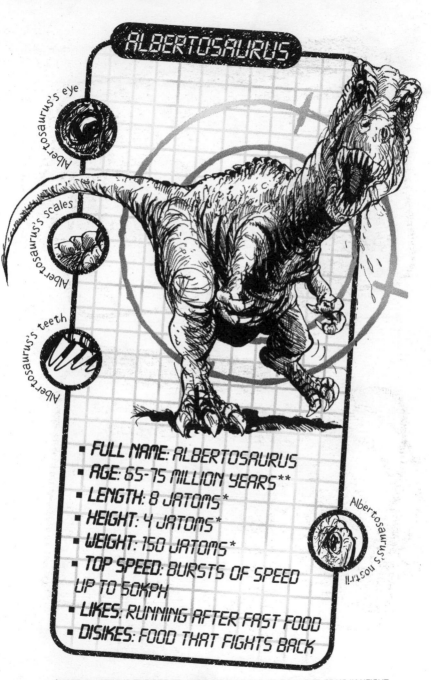

ALBERTOSAURUS

Albertosaurus's eye

Albertosaurus's scales

Albertosaurus's teeth

Albertosaurus's nostril

- **FULL NAME: ALBERTOSAURUS**
- **AGE: 65-75 MILLION YEARS****
- **LENGTH: 8 JATOMS***
- **HEIGHT: 4 JATOMS***
- **WEIGHT: 150 JATOMS***
- **TOP SPEED: BURSTS OF SPEED UP TO 50KPH**
- **LIKES: RUNNING AFTER FAST FOOD**
- **DISIKES: FOOD THAT FIGHTS BACK**

*NOTE: A JATOM IS THE SIZE OF JAMIE OR TOM: 125 CM TALL AND 27 KG IN WEIGHT
**NOTE: SCIENTISTS CALL THIS PERIOD THE LATE CRETACEOUS

DINOSAUR COVE

Village

Marina

Sealight Head

Landslips where clay and fossils are

Muddy beach

DINO CAVE

High Tide beach line

Low Tide beach line

Sea

Smuggler's Point

'Nacho, fetch!' Jamie Morgan yelled, pitching
a tennis ball along the sandy beach of
Dinosaur Cove.

The shaggy Old English sheepdog puppy
yapped joyfully as he raced after it.

'Nacho's faster than a speeding dino!' Tom
Clay declared.

Tom and Jamie grinned at each other. The
two friends knew just how speedy dinosaurs
could be—because they'd been chased by real
live ones! They'd discovered a secret cave in

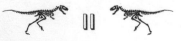

Dinosaur Cove
that led to an amazing
world full of awesome
prehistoric creatures.
That afternoon, they'd
been about to go back to
the Cretaceous for another
adventure when Grandad's
friend Agnes had asked them
to puppy-sit.

Nacho skidded to a
halt in a shower of sand.
He pounced on the ball
and sneezed.

N . . . n . . . *nach-oh!*

'Maybe that's why Agnes
called him Nacho,' Jamie joked
as the puppy picked up the ball
and hurtled back to them. He
dropped the slobbery, sandy ball

at Jamie's feet and gazed at him
with his head cocked to one side.

'Sit!' Jamie ordered. Nacho sat.
He was panting like a steam train
and so were the boys.

'Let's take a breather,' Tom said.
The boys plonked themselves on a ledge
next to a rock-pool.

'Lie down!' Jamie told Nacho. The puppy
curled up beside them.

'He's very well trained,' Tom said. 'Maybe
we could do some dino training with Wanna!'

'Awesome idea!' Jamie smiled, thinking
of the dinosaur friend
who always joined them
on their adventures.
'We'll try teaching
Wanna some tricks
when we get to the
Cretaceous.'

nach-oh!

Jamie took his notebook out of his backpack and opened it at the page where they'd drawn their map of Cretaceous Dino World.

'Where shall we explore this time?' Tom asked excitedly. 'Fang Rock or Misty Lagoon?'

Out of the corner of his eye, Jamie spotted a sudden movement at the base of the cliffs. Nacho's ears pricked up and he sprang to his feet—landing in the rock-pool.

Splash!

He bounded through
it, sploshing water all
over the boys, and took
off towards the cliffs.

'Nacho's chasing a
rabbit!' Jamie exclaimed,
stowing the notebook
in his backpack and
jumping up.

The boys set off
after him. 'Nacho!'
Tom shouted at
the top of
his lungs.
'Come back!'
But the puppy
carried on speeding
after the rabbit as
it zigzagged up the
steep cliffside.

The boys watched the rabbit bolt down
its hole.

Woof!

Nacho barked, sticking his nose down the
hole and wagging his tail excitedly.

Woof, woof, woof!

'Here, Nacho!' Tom commanded.

Nacho started scrabbling at the rabbit hole.

'I'll try to lure him back with one of
Agnes's treats,' Jamie said.

He rummaged through his backpack,
pushing aside his notebook, a Cretaceous
ammonite, a couple of empty doggy poo bags,

Woof, woof, woof!

a torch, and the
Fossil Finder.
His fingers closed
over a doggy chew
and he pulled it out,
tearing open the
plastic wrapper.

'Yurgh!' Jamie gagged. 'It smells like baby sick! Come and get your yummy snack, Nacho!' He waved the pongy treat in the puppy's direction.

Nacho turned and sniffed the air. Then he raced down to Jamie and sat at his feet, his tongue hanging out and drool dripping from his jaws. Jamie handed him the chew. Nacho gobbled his snack and licked his slobbery lips.

'He's like Wanna with his stinky gingko fruit,' Tom declared. 'I can't wait to see him again' he added.

'Not long now.' Jamie pointed to a woman coming along the beach, wearing a floppy hat. 'Here comes Agnes.'

Nacho yapped in delight and ran up to his owner, wagging his tail.

'Thanks for looking after him,' Agnes told the boys as she stroked Nacho's ears. 'I hope he wasn't any trouble—he often runs off. But I don't worry about him, as he always finds his way home again. You're a clever boy, aren't you?' She patted the puppy's furry back. 'His training's coming along nicely.'

'He does sit and fetch and roll over really well,' Tom agreed.

'And he walks to heel,' Agnes said proudly, adjusting her hat. 'Now I just need to teach

him to stop chasing things like cats and
squirrels . . . '

'And rabbits,' Jamie added with a smile.

Agnes looked at her watch. 'Time we
were getting back,' she said. 'Nacho likes his
afternoon nap. Enjoy the rest of the day.'

'Will do!' Tom assured her. He glanced
meaningfully at Jamie.

'Dino World here we come!'
Jamie whispered.

The boys waved goodbye
to Agnes and Nacho,
then turned and raced
up the steep cliff path
and boulders to

Smugglers' Cave. They squeezed through the
narrow gap at the back, into the secret cave
beyond. Jamie flicked on his torch and swept

the beam
of light over the
fossilized dino footprints
that led across the floor of the
cave towards what looked like a solid wall

of rock. Any minute now, they'd be passing straight through it!

He felt a surge of anticipation as he fitted his foot into the first of the three-toed prints, but before he could take the next step, a scritch-scratching noise of claws on stone came from behind them.

Jamie dropped his torch in surprise.

'There's something in the cave!' he whispered as the light went out.

CHAPTER 2

SEARCH:
ABCDEFGHIJKLMN
OPQRSTUVWXYZ
1234567890

In the pitch dark, Jamie and Tom listened to
the snuffling and scrabbling noises coming
from the other side of the gap they had
crawled through.

'What if something's escaped from Dino
World?' Tom whispered.

'It can't be from Dino World,' Jamie
hissed as noisy sniffs echoed round the secret
cave. 'It would have turned to dust, like
that gingko we tried to bring back.' He
stepped out of the fossil footprints, groped

around for his torch and switched it on, shining it on the gap.

'It could be a badger or a fox, then,' Tom said in a low voice. 'They can be fierce if they're cornered. I hope it doesn't find us . . . '

Sniff!

The sound was louder. The creature growled and scrabbled some more at the stone.

'Sounds like a wolf that's got out of the wildlife park,' Jamie whispered nervously.

SNIFF!

A hairy snout poked through the gap.

'It's coming for us!' Tom gasped, hurriedly

stepping into the stone footprints. 'Quick!
Let's get into Dino World and leave it behind.'

There was a flash of light as Tom
disappeared. Jamie followed close behind.
As he stepped towards the last fossilized print,
he turned and shone his torch behind him.

A hairy creature hurled itself
into the beam of light. It was on
him in an instant. Jamie lurched
forward under the creature's
weight, and his foot
landed heavily
in the final
footprint.

There was another tremendous flash, and Jamie fell onto the warm spongy ground inside Gingko Cave, with the creature on top of him.

Yip, yip, yip!

It barked excitedly, licking his face with its wet pink tongue.

'Nacho!' Tom laughed. 'Jamie thought you were a wolf. That makes him a wombat!'

'Nacho's great-great-great-great-great-great-grandfather *might* have been a wolf,' Jamie said indignantly, pushing the fluffy puppy off his chest.

'You'd need a lot more greats than that,' Tom said. 'A wolf would have to evolve *a lot* to turn into Nacho!'

Jamie jumped to his feet, brushing off dead pine needles, bits of fern, and gingko  leaves. He breathed in the warm moist air and the compost-like smell of the Cretaceous jungle. The air hummed with

the noise of a zillion buzzing insects. It was
fantastic to be back in the Cretaceous.

Nacho's tail wagged excitedly as he stuck
his nose into the layer of leaf mould that
covered the ground and snuffled deeply.

N-nach-ho!
He sneezed.
'Cool!'
Jamie said. 'He's
the first ever dog
in Dino World!'

'We're going to have to keep a close eye on
him,' Tom murmured.

Woof! Nacho's tail stopped wagging and
stuck straight into the air. He put his nose
to the ground and bounded off into the ferns
that grew between the gingko trees.

'He's picked up a scent,' Jamie groaned.

'Nacho! Come back!' the boys yelled as
they hurtled after him.

The puppy scampered back and forth
between the gingko trees, his nose skimming
over the sludgy fruits that had splattered
down from the trees.

'What's he tracking?' Tom panted.

'Dunno. All I can smell is gingko stink.'
Jamie skidded on a pool of gingko slime that
looked and smelt like rotten carrot sludge.

Ahead of them, Nacho had stopped at a
fern-covered clearing in the trees.

Woof woof woof!

A bony head poked out of
the ferns, followed by an upright
lizard-like body.

The dinosaur wagged its scaly tail.

Grunk?

'Wanna!' Jamie and
Tom exclaimed.

Their dinosaur friend glanced
nervously at the barking puppy.
Then he trotted out of the ferns
towards Jamie and Tom. But
before he could reach them,
Nacho bounded up to the
little wannanosaurus.

Grunk?

Wanna froze. His tail drooped as the sheepdog puppy ran circles around him. 'He's never seen a dog before,' Jamie commented. 'He doesn't know what to make of him.'

Nacho crouched down in front of Wanna, his tail thumping the ground.

Yip, yip, yip.

'Nacho wants to play,' Tom chuckled.

'I don't think Wanna does,' Jamie said.

Nacho sprang up on his back legs and tried to pounce on Wanna. The dinosaur grunked in alarm and lowered his bony skull in self-defence. Nacho ran into it.

Aooo!

Nacho howled, bouncing off Wanna's hard
head. He ran behind Tom's legs.

Grunk,
grunk,
grunk!

Wanna skittered across to Jamie
and hid behind him.

Jamie and Tom looked at
each other.

'What a pair of
wombats,' Jamie
chuckled. 'Now we
have to help a dog
and a dino make
friends.'

CHAPTER 3

Jamie twisted round and patted Wanna on his
scaly nose.

'It's OK, Wanna,' he murmured. 'Nacho's
a friend.'

Wanna's tail twitched and he stuck his head
out from behind the shelter of Jamie's body.

Tom squatted down and stroked Nacho's
ears. Then he took hold of Nacho's collar and
slowly coaxed him towards Jamie and Wanna.

Nacho stretched his nose towards the
little dinosaur.

Jamie held his breath as the
two creatures slowly moved towards
each other. Finally, Wanna bumped
his cool scaly dino muzzle against
Nacho's warm rubbery nose,
surrounded by its halo
of fluffy hair. Their
tails began to wag.
     'That's it—
make friends!'
Jamie said.

Wanna
trotted in a
circle around
the puppy. Nacho
began to sniff at the
dino's bottom.
     N-acho!
Nacho sneezed.
Grunk!

Wanna leapt
into the air in
surprise.

'Imagine if we
made friends like
that!' Tom snorted with
laughter.

'At least it's working,' Jamie
chuckled as Wanna gently nudged
the sheepdog puppy. Nacho raced
round the little dino, nipping playfully
at his toes, making him hop from foot to foot.

'Better make this a quick visit to Dino
World,' Tom told Jamie as they watched
Wanna and Nacho tumble around the ferns.
'We have to get Nacho home for his nap
before Agnes starts worrying.'

'We'll just stay long enough to get Nacho
to help us teach Wanna some dog tricks,'
Jamie agreed.

Tom grinned. 'He's already started—look!'

At the edge of the ferns, Wanna was watching Nacho roll in gingko goo.

Grunk!

Wanna lowered his head and rubbed his cheek into the pongy sludge, then he pivoted on his shoulder and landed on his back with a glubby splat.

'Maybe this isn't the best place for dino training,' Jamie groaned as Wanna and Nacho gleefully kicked their back legs up in the air, writhing in the stinky slime.

'Let's take 'em to the Great Plains for a bit,' Tom said. 'There's more space there.'

'Awesome idea!' Jamie picked a handful of firm gingko fruit from a nearby tree. 'Here, Wanna!' he called.

The dino leapt to his feet and dashed up to him. Jamie handed him a gingko and put the rest in his backpack.

'Gingkoes are great dino training treats,' Tom commented, as Wanna chomped noisily.

Nacho ran up, his fur matted with gingko grunge. He licked at the slobbery juice that dripped down Wanna's chin. His furry muzzle wrinkled and he spat it out.

'He only likes gingkoes on his outside, not his inside!' Tom laughed.

'Come on, you two stinkbombs; we're going to the Great Plains.' Jamie pulled out the compass from his backpack.

'That's north, across the river,' Tom reminded him.

Jamie lined up the compass arrow with north and the four of them set off, scrambling down the steep slopes of Gingko Hill, into the Cretaceous jungle. They pushed through the long emerald-green creepers that hung down from the tall conifer trees and dodged around the tightly packed ferns. The warm rich smell of damp leaf mould welled up around them, and here and there the jungle greens were splashed with the bright yellows, purples, and oranges of slimy fungi that sprouted from rotting tree trunks. Nacho

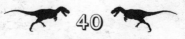

40

barked as
a millipede as
long as he was
scuttled across his path.
'Shhh!' Tom warned. 'We're right
by the river where dinos come to drink.
We don't want a meat-eater to hear us!'

Jamie cautiously pushed through a curtain
of creepers and caught his breath. Not far
upriver, a duck-billed dinosaur was standing
at the water's edge. It was dappled green,
like the jungle.

'Coast's clear of meat-eaters,' Jamie
said, beckoning to Tom, Wanna, and
Nacho to come closer. 'But there's an
awesome plant-eater.'

The dino was the size of a bus and it had
a rounded bony crest at the back of its head.
They watched as it bent down and pulled out
a bunch of waterweed in its duck-bill-shaped

mouth. They were so close they could hear
chomping and slushing noises as it mashed
up and swallowed the weed.

'What is it?' Tom whispered.

Jamie fished out the Fossil Finder and
switched it on. The Happy Hunting screen

popped up and he typed in *'DUCK BILL WITH CREST'*. He scrolled through the list until he found a picture of a matching dino.

'CORY-THO-SAUR-US,' he read. *'A MEMBER OF THE HADROSAUR FAMILY WITH HUNDREDS OF PLANT-MASHING TEETH.'*

The cory's stomach gurgled as it bent forward to take another mouthful of weed. Wanna grunked impatiently and walked off downstream, where the river was wider and full of rocks. He stepped carefully from one rock to another.

'Wanna's found a place to cross, come on!' Jamie packed away the Fossil Finder.

The boys hopped from rock to rock across the shallow river.

Yip!

Nacho yelped excitedly and threw himself into the water. In no time at all, he swam to the other side and scrambled up the bank.

'Watch out, he's going to soak us!' Tom yelled.

The ball of damp fluff shook himself from nose to tail, splattering Jamie, Tom, and Wanna with water drops.

'At least he doesn't stink so much now,' Jamie muttered as they stepped out of the green jungle into the shimmering heat of the open plains.

Tom jumped up on a boulder. He wiped the water marks off the lenses of his binoculars with his T-shirt, and put them to his eyes.

'No meat-eaters,' he said, jumping down and handing Jamie the binoculars, 'but check out the alamosaurs.'

Jamie scanned the Great Plains from right to left. Fang Rock and the Far Away Mountains were bathed in a shimmering heat haze. He twisted further to his left and surveyed the edge of the jungle.

'I see 'em!' Jamie exclaimed. 'Cool!'

He focused the binoculars on the group of heavyweight plant-eaters in the distance. As he watched, the alamosaurs turned their long necks and sniffed the air, then went back to grazing on the tops of the trees.

'They don't look as if anything's worrying them. I reckon it's safe to do some dino training,' Jamie declared, handing the binoculars back to Tom.

'Nacho can demonstrate,' Tom said. 'Sit, Nacho!' He pointed at him.

Nacho sat.

'Good dog,' said Tom, patting him on the head. 'Sit, Wanna!'

Jamie pointed at the little dino.

Wanna turned to look behind him and his tail swept round and hit Jamie on the nose.

'Sit!' Jamie pressed down on Wanna's back.

Wanna wagged his tail and whacked him round the ear.

'I wouldn't hire you as a dino trainer,' Tom said with a giggle. 'Wanna hasn't got a clue how to sit. Let me try something else.'

Jamie rubbed his nose and ear as Tom took a gingko out of the backpack and walked a few paces away.

'Nacho, come!' Tom shouted.

Nacho raced up to him and stood at his feet, panting eagerly. Tom ruffled his ears.

'Wanna, come!' Tom squatted on his heels and held out the gingko.

Wanna rushed towards Tom and knocked him flat on the ground in his eagerness to get at the stinky fruit.

'Great training technique,' Jamie chortled as his friend staggered to his feet.

A sudden *arooop!* interrupted him.

It was followed quickly by calls like a cross between a sheep's bleat and a cow's bellow, which echoed around the plains.

'Ankies!' Tom exclaimed in delight as a herd of ankylosaurs trooped out of the jungle and headed towards them.

'It's great to see them again,' Jamie agreed, remembering the time they had rescued a baby anky from a swamp and helped it get back to its herd.

Nacho crept close to Jamie's side as the huge spiky-headed herbivores rumbled past them like tanks on legs, swinging the bony clubs on the ends of their tails. Wanna watched them as he chomped up his gingko treat.

'There are a lot more babies this time,'

Tom said, pointing out a group of young ankies the size of go-carts. 'I hope they don't attract any predat—'

Guuuur!

The roar echoed across the plains.

Jamie grabbed the binoculars. There was no sign of the alamosaurs. Something else

was moving between the
trees. His blood ran cold
as a gigantic two-legged
dino with fangs like steak
knives stepped out of the
jungle. It gave a great
snort and thundered
towards them.

'Quick! Hide!' Jamie ran behind a heap of boulders, closely followed by Tom, Wanna, and Nacho. They peeped through the cracks between the rocks. The enormous killer lizard was charging towards the herd of ankies.

'It's not a T-Rex,' Tom murmured. 'It's more streamlined and athletic-looking.'

'And faster,' Jamie murmured. He grabbed the Fossil Finder and tapped in *'CRETACEOUS PREDATORS'*.

'*ALBERTOSAURUS*. That's it.' Jamie skimmed the page quickly. '*BURSTS OF SPEED*,' he murmured. '*KEEN SENSE OF SMELL* . . . '

He stowed the Fossil Finder and peered through a crack, just in time to see the albertosaurus charge into the herd of ankies.

Aroop!

They scattered out of its way. The vicious carnivore paused for a moment, drool dripping from its fangs.

'It's hungry,' Tom murmured. Beside him, Wanna froze. Nacho's fur began to bristle.

Aroop!

The biggest anky took a swipe at the albie with its club. There was a *thwack!* as it connected with the predator's tail.

Gurrrrrr!

The albie roared with rage and lunged at the anky. The baby ankies squeaked piteously and raced off in all directions.

The big anky turned.

Thwack!

Its club hit its target again, sending the predator staggering.

Thwack!

Gurrrr!

The albie slunk towards the jungle, taking backward glances at the ankies.

'It can't risk having a leg broken by the anky's club,' Tom whispered. 'It'd die of starvation if it couldn't hunt.' He trained his binoculars on the spot where the albie had disappeared into the jungle. 'I can see ferns moving,' Tom murmured. 'It's still lurking.'

'The baby ankies have scattered all over the place,' Jamie said worriedly, pointing them out. 'They'll be easy pickings for any carnivore.'

Nacho's eyes followed his gestures.
He pricked up his ears.

Woof!

He dashed across the plains.

'Nacho! Come back!' Jamie and Tom
yelled.

Gak-gak-gak-gak-gak.

It sounded as if Wanna was trying to call
him back, too.

Nacho raced towards the furthest
baby anky and darted at the dino's ankles.
It skittered away from him, towards the anky
herd, which was slowly moving back together.

'He's rounding the ankies up, like they're
sheep!' Jamie exclaimed.

'Well, he is a sheepdog, fossil features,'
Tom said with a grin as the puppy turned his
attention to another baby anky.

Grunk!
Wanna bounded towards a third baby anky and gently butted it towards the rest of the herd.

Tom glanced towards the jungle. 'It's not just the baby ankies who are in danger now. The albie might attack Wanna or Nacho before they manage to herd them all.'

'You're right,' Jamie agreed. 'There's only one way we can speed things up.'

He and Tom looked at each other, then jumped out from the boulder and ran for the nearest baby anky.

'Shoo!' Jamie yelled, holding his arms open wide.

'Shoo!' Tom echoed. 'Shoo! Shoo!'

The little anky took one look at the boys and scuttled towards the safety of the herd.

Soon all the ankies had been rounded up.

'Yay! We've got them back together!' Jamie took the binoculars and scrambled onto a big boulder to check the jungle for signs of the albertosaurus.

He looked back across the herd of ankies just in time to see the predator's tail disappear into the jungle.

'I think the albie's given up,' he said, and breathed a sigh of relief.

'It's too scared to attack the ankies now they've regrouped,' Tom said as Nacho and Wanna bounded up, panting and wagging their tails. 'We're all safe now,' he said, and gave Jamie a high five.

'Go, dino team!' Jamie grinned. He rummaged in his backpack and found a chew for the puppy and a gingko for the dinosaur. Nacho and Wanna gobbled down their treats.

'That was exciting, but now it's time we got Nacho back to Agnes,' Tom reminded Jamie as the little dino and the puppy licked their sticky lips. 'I know she said he runs away sometimes, but we don't want her to be worried about him.'

'Definitely not.' Jamie hoisted up his backpack. The boulder wobbled as he jumped down from it, and a rabbit-sized dino shot out from underneath.

It had a V-shaped crest on its head that from the side looked like bunny ears.

'It's a baby lambeosaurus,' Jamie muttered. 'I recognize the crest from the Fossil Finder.'

Yip! Yip! Yip!

Nacho bolted after it.

'Oh no!' Tom groaned. 'He's run off after a dino-rabbit!'

CHAPTER 5

SEARCH:

'Come back, Nacho!' Jamie yelled.

Grunk!

Wanna lifted his scaly snout into the air.

Nacho glanced back at them, but carried on running.

'Sit!' Tom tried.

Wanna sat down obediently. But Nacho was still pelting after the dino-rabbit, in the direction of Fang Rock.

'Heel!' Jamie shrieked, sprinting off after the puppy. Wanna ran along next to him.

'Wanna *can* do dog tricks.' Tom panted, racing along beside them.

The dino-rabbit was heading towards the loop in the river, with Nacho snapping at its heels. The ground beneath their feet was getting soggier and soggier.

'Watch out, it's boggy here,' Jamie groaned.

Ahead of them, the lightly built dino-rabbit scuttled across the muddy ground as if it was solid rock. Close on its trail, Nacho was jumping over stagnant boggy puddles, using clumps of ferns like stepping stones.

Jamie and Wanna leapt into the air like hurdlers, both aiming for the same small clump of ferns.

Whump!

They bounced off each other and landed in a pool of stinky mud.

Splat!

The mud glooped and glubbed as they struggled to their feet.

'Having fun wallowing, you pair of prehistoric hippos?' Tom chuckled, jumping

carefully from one fern clump to another.
The spiral tendrils of a new fern frond tangled
round his trainers, knotting his feet together.

Splat!

Tom landed in the mud and came up
snorting.

'Now who's a prehistoric hippo?' Jamie
laughed wryly.

The boys and Wanna waded through the
gloopy goo and out onto firmer ground, just in
time to see Nacho chase the dino-rabbit up to
a weathered rock the size of a house. Nacho
ran behind the rock, barking wildly.

There was a sudden yelp and Nacho came
shooting out again, his tail between his legs.
He glanced back over his shoulder,
shaking all over.

'*Uh-oh!*' Tom groaned
as a huge dino with three
fearsome-looking horns

and a sharp beaked mouth emerged from
behind the rock. 'He's disturbed a triceratops,
and it doesn't look happy!'

Jamie caught his breath. T-tops might be a plant-eater, but it was bigger than the biggest elephant at the zoo. Nacho stood rooted to the spot as the T-tops tossed its head and snorted with rage at the trembling puppy.

'It looks like a bull getting ready to charge!' Tom muttered.

The ground trembled as the T-tops stamped its feet.

'Nacho will get flattened,' Jamie whispered nervously.

Suddenly there was a loud *Gak!*

Tom and Jamie glanced at each other.

Wanna was revving up.

Gak! Gak! Gak!

Their dino friend kicked at the ground.

The T-tops's black eyes shifted

from Nacho to Wanna.
It tilted the huge frill at the
back of its neck towards the
little dino. Its three horns
faced forwards like
deadly lances.

Wanna stopped
kicking his feet. He
lowered his bony
head and stiffened
as if bracing
himself for impact.

'Wanna hasn't got a
chance against a T-tops,'
Jamie shouted. 'We have
to stop it charging
into him!'

CHAPTER 6

'Distract it!' Jamie yelled, shrugging off his backpack and pulling his muddy T-shirt over his head. Tom whipped off his T-shirt, too.

The two friends stood next to each other and waved their T-shirts at the angry triceratops, like matadors waving their capes at a bull.

The huge beast thundered towards them, its horns level with the boys' chests. In the nick of time, Jamie and Tom leapt aside, and the T-tops charged between them. Its sharp horns tore the T-shirts out of the boys' hands.

They flapped over the dino's eyes, temporarily blinding it.

'That was close!' Jamie muttered.

The three-horned dino skidded to a halt and tossed its head, shaking off the boys' T-shirts.

Nacho cautiously slunk up behind the huge dinosaur and grabbed Tom's T-shirt in his jaws.

Wanna watched with his head on one side as the puppy returned the T-shirt to Tom and sat down obediently next to him.

Jamie's mouth dropped open as Wanna scuttled across to fetch his T-shirt.

'Awesome retrieving, Wanna,' Jamie whispered as Wanna dropped the shirt at his feet.

Tom and Jamie gripped their T-shirts in both hands, ready for the grumpy dino to turn and charge again. But the triceratops had lost interest in them. It was staring into the distance.

Tom, Jamie, and Wanna followed its gaze. The Far Away Mountains were shrouded in a weird

reddish-brown layer of fog that they hadn't
noticed before.

The T-tops snorted and stomped off across
the Plains. Wanna shifted from foot to foot,
grunking nervously.

'Maybe there's a storm brewing,' Tom said,
pulling his T-shirt over his head. 'Let's get
Nacho back home while he's being good.'

'Before he finds anything else to chase!'
Jamie agreed, putting on his shirt. It was

caked with mud and dino drool and there was a tear in it from the T-tops's horn. He picked up his backpack.

As they trekked into the jungle, Nacho began to growl.

Grrrr!

He was quiet at first, then grew louder and louder.

Jamie looked at Tom. 'I don't think it's the storm that's bothering him . . . '

GURRRRR!

A roar came from the trees straight ahead of them. The albie burst out, snarling ferociously.

Tom gulped as it sped towards them. 'It's been tracking us.'

'We can't outrun that!' cried Jamie. He stared in horror as the muscular long-legged carnivore quickly narrowed the gap between them.

Woof!

Nacho leapt to his feet and crouched in the albie's path, barking loudly. The boys watched, appalled, as the albertosaurus

lunged
at the
puppy,
gnashing its
crocodile-like jaws.

Yip!

Nacho yelped.
He flung himself onto
his back, rolling over and over.

Jamie's heart skipped a beat. Was the albie
going to scrunch him up? But as the predator
lunged down at Nacho, jaws gaping
wide, the puppy jumped to
his feet and ran in tight
circles around the
albie's legs.

Yip!

The albie
twisted this
way and that,
snapping its fangs
at the quick-
moving puppy.
Suddenly,
Nacho broke
away and dashed
towards the
double prongs of
Fang Rock. The
albertosaurus snatched at him, but
missed. It lurched drunkenly from one foot
to the other.

'Nacho's made it dizzy,' Tom hissed as the
scaly predator tottered about. 'Let's get out of
here before it gets its balance back.'

Jamie, Tom, and Wanna raced after Nacho.
Jamie glanced back over his shoulder and saw

the albie staggering behind them,
veering from side to side.
'It's catching up!' he yelled.

They hurtled over the ferns and
pushed through the few straggly
creepers that hung down from
the closest corner of Fang Rock.
They pelted behind it, but
could still hear the albie
gaining ground.

Nacho huddled between
the two pointy rocks, panting
and exhausted. Jamie, Tom,
and Wanna skidded to a
halt beside him.

The albie's head appeared
round the side of the rock.

Gurrrrrr!

It growled, showing
its knife-like fangs.

Jamie looked around wildly, but there was
nowhere to hide—and if they ran, the albie
would easily catch them. Wanna hurled
himself at the rockface, but it was
too smooth and too steep to
climb. He slid back down
and huddled beside
Jamie, Tom, and
Nacho.

GURRRRR!

The albertosaurus roared triumphantly.

Nacho and Wanna
started to whimper.

'We're trapped,' said Jamie.
A blast of the albie's breath hit him
in the face, and he gagged at the
stench of rotten meat.

'We're dinner!' Tom
muttered.

CHAPTER 7

The albertosaurus thrust its head through
the V-shaped prongs of rock. It towered over
them, taller than a telegraph pole. Jamie,
Tom, Wanna, and Nacho held their breath
as the vicious carnivore bent towards them,
saliva dripping from its fangs.

A scaly nostril brushed across the top of
Jamie's head. The albie was sniffing at each
of them in turn. Would it gobble them down
in one gulp, or chomp them up bit by bit?
Which one of them would it eat first?

Jamie
closed his
eyes . . .

From high above his
head he heard a great roar.
'That's not the albie,'
shouted Tom.

Jamie opened his eyes again
and peered upwards. All he
could see was the creamy-orange
scales of the albie's throat. It was
sniffing at the air, twisting its great
jaws from side to side. Slimy strings
of drool swung from its fangs.

Gurrr!

The albie growled. Its muscular tail thwacked against the side of Fang Rock like a whip as it turned and ran away.

'We're alive!' Jamie and Tom leapt up and down, clapping each other on the back and patting Wanna and Nacho. Their dino and doggy friends skipped around, joyfully wagging their tails and trying to lick the boys and each other.

'Why didn't it eat us?' Jamie asked as the excitement died down.

'It could smell something,' Tom said slowly. 'Maybe something scared it off . . . '

Jamie gulped. What would scare off an albertosaurus? He glanced around nervously.

91

Wanna raised his scaly snout, like the albie had done, and sniffed at the air.

Grunk, grunk, grunk!

He stretched out his neck and tail as if he was about to run, too.

Tom and Jamie exchanged glances. Then they cautiously edged round the base of Fang Rock, rounding a clump of ferns.

Whoosh!

A gust of sand-laden wind hit them in the face.

Jamie put his hand over his eyes and peered through his fingers. Ahead was what looked like a mile-high wall of reddish brown fog rolling towards them. Only it wasn't fog at all.

'It's a sandstorm!' Tom choked as the wind swirled round Fang Rock. 'And it's coming our way.'

92

Whoosh!

Zillions of tiny
particles lashed at them. Jamie's face felt as
if it was being sandpapered.

Grunk!

Wanna backed into the clump of dusty
ferns, closely followed by a sneezing Nacho.

'Wanna's got the right idea. Take cover!'
Tom coughed, dropping to his knees and
crawling into the ferns. Jamie did the same.
Grains of sand were pinging off the ferns like
drops of rain hitting a flat rock.

'Wanna!' Jamie yelled above the whirling wind. 'Nacho! Where are you?'

Grunk!

Woof!

The answering calls seemed to come from inside Fang Rock.

Jamie and Tom crawled out of the other side of the dust-battered ferns. Wanna and Nacho were huddled up together in a shallow crevice in the base of the rock. The boys wriggled their way in beside them.

Outside, the ferns were being buffeted by gale-force winds. The hot air was filling with dust and sand, making it hard to breathe.

'Cover your mouth and nose!' Tom said. He pulled his T-shirt over the lower part of his face.

Jamie shrugged off his backpack and did the same. Behind him, Wanna stuck his snout under the backpack. Nacho curled up under Tom's legs.

Something scuttled into the cave.

Woof!

Nacho barked.

'Uh-oh,' Jamie muttered.

It was another baby lambeosaurus, looking for somewhere

to shelter from the sandstorm. But the dino-rabbit took one look at Nacho, then turned and fled.

Woof! Woof! Woof!

Nacho leaped
to his feet.
'You're staying here!'
Tom grabbed at the puppy's
collar, but he twisted out of his
way and bolted after the little dinosaur.

'He's gone again,' Tom despaired.

'And he's picked the worst time to run off,' added Jamie.

He scrambled to his knees and crawled through the ferns, feeling the whoosh of the sandy wind. He pulled his T-shirt up over his face and squinted through the hole made by the T-tops's horn. The dust and sand stung his eyes as he peered into the wind. Visibility was

down to about the length of a football pitch.
He could just make out Nacho running north-
east, on the edge of the dust cloud, chasing
the dino-rabbit towards a tall rocky pillar.

There was a surge of sandy dust and the
sky darkened. It was impossible to see the
difference between the earth and sky. Nacho
and the lambeosaurus were swallowed up by
the red-brown fog.

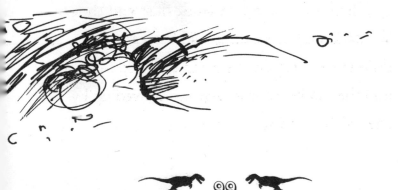

Jamie crawled back to the rocky shelter.
'There's no way we can chase him in
this,' he yelled, raising his voice against the
shrieking wind. 'Nacho's gone!'

The sandstorm howled round Fang Rock like a ravening beast.

Jamie, Tom, and Wanna huddled together in their rocky shelter. They looked at each other worriedly.

'All we can do is wait it out,' Tom shouted in Jamie's ear.

'You're right. But it's horrible not knowing where he is,' Jamie groaned, gazing out of the shelter.

Gusts of sand blew into the shelter, making

their eyes sting. Jamie pulled his T-shirt more
closely round his face, and Tom did the same.

Splurgh-grunk!

Wanna spat out a mouthful of sand.

'You can't breathe properly either, can you?'
Tom said to the little dinosaur. He felt around
in his pocket, pulled out a handkerchief and
wrapped it over Wanna's mouth and
nostrils. He knotted it at the
back of Wanna's head. The
wannanosaurus gave a muffled
grunk and curled up between
the two boys.

They sat in worried
silence until at last the
roaring sound faded and the sky lightened.
Jamie, Tom, and Wanna emerged from
their shelter. The boys pulled their T-shirts
away from their faces and Wanna shook
away the handkerchief. Tom stuffed it back

in his pocket. The clump of ferns had been beaten flat and everything, including Fang Rock, was covered with a thick gritty layer of red sand. As they walked, their feet stirred up the dust, making Wanna sneeze.

Nach-oh! spluttered the little dinosaur.
'Wanna sounds like he's calling for him,'
Tom said. 'Good idea, Wanna!'

Both boys shouted at the top of their lungs. 'Nacho! Nacho!' But trails of sand still drifted in the air, tickling the backs of their throats. They doubled over in fits of coughing.

Wanna looked around, grunking sadly. There was no sign of the little sheepdog.

Tom knelt down to examine the sand-strewn ground. 'No way can we track him,' he said in dismay. 'The sandstorm's blasted away his paw prints. He could be miles away by now.'

Nacho! Nacho!

'The albie might come back and eat him,' Jamie said worriedly. A panicky feeling welled up inside him. 'How

would we explain *that* to Agnes
and Grandad? We have to
find him!'

'Where did you last see him?'
Tom asked.

'Heading that way.' Jamie
pointed to the rocky pillar.
'Maybe he's still there.
Come on!'

They hurried towards the
pillar. Its surface was twisted
and pockmarked, as if it had
been blasted by countless
sandstorms. Jamie's heart beat
faster as they skidded to a
halt beside it. In front of
the pillar, the land dropped
away into a hidden canyon.

It was a sunken valley with
steep slopes, filled with a jumble

of rocky towers, spires, and pillars. Each had horizontal stripes made from different types of stone, coloured in every shade of red and gold and eroded into weird and wonderful shapes.

'That one looks like a giant sheep,' Jamie said, pointing it out.

'And there's a skyscraper.' Tom indicated another rock.

The hundreds of rocky formations were so close together that it was hard to see a way between them.

'It's a maze,'
Tom declared.
'An a-maze-ing maze!'
Jamie groaned as
Tom guffawed.

Wanna put his head to one side.
'Shhh!' Jamie hissed. 'Wanna
can hear something.'

The boys cupped their hands to
their ears and listened intently.

'*Woof!*'

The bark was faint but unmistakable.
Jamie's heart leapt with joy. 'Nacho!'

He hurtled down the steep rocky slope
into the canyon, Tom and Wanna beside him.

The bizarre rocks towered above them,
blotting out the light and casting spooky
shadows. Narrow sand-blown pathways twisted
and turned between the crazy formations.

Woof! Woof! Woof!

Nacho's bark echoed off
the canyon walls. It was
impossible to pinpoint
where it was
coming from.

'Nacho!' Tom and Jamie yelled again.

Cho . . . cho . . . cho . . .

The shadowy canyon echoed back
their call.

A shiver ran down Jamie's spine.

How would they ever find Nacho in here?

CHAPTER 9

SEARCH:

'Maybe Wanna can sniff him out,' Tom
suggested. He got down on his hands and
knees and sniffed at the ground to show
Wanna what he meant. 'Woof!' Tom barked,
wiggling his bottom from side to side, as if he
was wagging a tail. 'Woof! Woof!'

Wanna stared at him in disbelief.

Jamie dropped to his knees and crawled
after Tom, sniffing loudly.

For a moment Wanna stood looking at
them as if they'd gone mad, but then their

dinosaur friend dropped his snout and began
to sniff too.

'That's it, Wanna,' Jamie encouraged him.
Sniff . . . sniff . . . sniff . . .

Wanna snuffled. Then he raced up to
Jamie and nudged at his backpack.

'He doesn't get it,' Jamie groaned, standing
up. 'He's sniffing out gingkoes.'

'I'll give him one.' Tom stood up as well
and put his hand into the backpack. 'Yuck!'
he spluttered as the ripe fruit squished

between his fingers. Stinky gingko juice
dripped all over the backpack and ran down
Tom's arm to his elbow.

Tom held out the fruit to Wanna, who
wagged his tail in delight as he
gobbled it up then slurped
the stinky slime off Tom.
The smell of ripe gingko
lingered around them. Jamie
screwed up his face in disgust.
'Wanna might not be able to smell
Nacho, but he can definitely smell us,' he
groaned.

'That's it!' Tom said with a grin. 'We'll
never be able to find Nacho in this
maze—so he can sniff us out
instead!'

'Yes!' Jamie exclaimed.
'We can lure him to us with
a smelly treat, like we did

Urgh!

when he was chasing that rabbit on the beach.' He pulled a doggy treat out of his backpack and ripped open the packet.

'He can't resist these . . .'

Jamie waved the chew stick about. Its baby-sick pong welled around them. A sudden breeze blew the stench back in his face.

'Urgh!' he gagged.

Tom stuck his finger in his mouth so it was wet, then held it up. The breeze cooled the right side of it.

'The wind's coming from that way,' he said, pointing to the right—deeper among the rocky maze. 'If we go there we'll be upwind, and the breeze can carry the dog treat scent to Nacho. Then he'll sniff us out.'

They set off into the maze. It was cooler
than on the plains, and like being in a dense
fairytale forest—but with rocks instead

of trees. The sort of fairytale forest where witches and wolves might hang out . . .

'What's that?' Jamie jumped as a long dark shape skittered across a twisted turret of rock.

'Your shadow, you wombat,' Tom said with a nervous laugh.

Something small and lizardy shot across the path in front of them, too fast for them to make out what it was.

Jamie half-expected to see Nacho flying after it, but instead of a bark, an unearthly *creech* echoed around them. Jamie's blood ran cold. It was unmistakably a hunting cry.

Wanna grunked and looked up, fidgeting from foot to foot.

'Is it a pterodactyl?' Jamie murmured, gazing into the sky.

Creech!

The scary sound came again. It was at ground level.

Tom turned to Jamie. 'Dinosaur!' he murmured. 'A meat-eater lives in this maze!'

Jamie could see that under the

mud and freckles, his friend's face had gone pale. He gulped. 'Let's hope Nacho finds us before it does,' he said, wafting the smelly dog chew from side to side. 'And before it finds him.'

'Try not to make any noise,' Tom advised.

They tiptoed through the twisting, turning maze of strange shadowy rocks, glancing anxiously from side to side.

A patter of claws came from the far side of a rocky tower.

'Nacho!' Jamie breathed, hurrying towards the sound.

But it wasn't a dog that appeared round the rock. It was a feathered two-legged dinosaur, as tall as a giraffe, with a snout lined with pointy fangs. The dino's shaggy blue-green feathers shimmered in the shadowy

light and the sharp talons on its feet pattered against the ground as it stalked towards them.

'It's a raptor!' Tom yelled.

'Run!'

CHAPTER 10

Jamie, Tom, and Wanna raced through the maze of rocks with the giant raptor on their heels.

Jamie glanced behind to see it fan out a crest of purple feathers and lunge feet first towards them with a blood-curdling *creech!*

In the nick of time, the boys and Wanna swung round a pillar of rock and flattened their backs against it. Ahead of them, the path forked into two passageways. The raptor

shot past, and raced up the passageway
on the right.

'It hasn't seen us,' Tom breathed as he,
Jamie, and Wanna turned down the other
path and squeezed past a boulder the shape
of a giant turtle.

On one side of the path rose the steep wall of
stone that formed the edge of the canyon.

Woof!

A loud happy bark bounced off the
canyon wall. Jamie didn't know
whether to laugh or cry.

Nacho was
nearby—but he was
making so much noise
that the raptor would
be able to find them!
'Nacho! Shhh!' he hissed.
The sheepdog puppy emerged from
the shadows and gambolled towards
him, enthusiastically wagging his tail.

His eyes were fixed firmly on the treat that Jamie was still clutching in his hand.

Woof! Woof!

He barked joyfully.

Tom peered back round the turtle-shaped rock. The raptor's glittering eyes stared back at him.

'It's found us!' he groaned. There was a sudden swishing of feathers and a clattering of claws as the raptor sprang onto the turtle-shaped rock.

Nacho looked up in amazement. He howled, dashing off with his tail between his legs. He shot into the shadows at the base of the rocky wall of the canyon, and disappeared into a hole.

'Follow him!' Jamie yelled.

The giant raptor leapt into the air like a long-jumper. Jamie sprinted after Nacho,

and did a rugby dive into the hole. Wanna and Tom dived in after him. When the feathered predator tried to follow them, it clattered against the narrow opening.

'Way to go, Nacho!' Jamie cheered. He glanced around. The hole opened into a cave

the size of a small car. 'We'd never have found this on our own,' he said.

The raptor's long claw came through the hole and sliced across the cave like a meat cleaver.

'Watch out!' Tom shrieked.

They leapt over the vicious claw as it swept backwards and forwards in the confined space. It was like skipping with a deadly rope. The raptor withdrew its claw.

Creech!

The raptor's terrible cry echoed round the tiny cave. It stuck its feathery head through the hole.

Jamie, Tom, and Wanna flattened themselves against the rock.

The raptor fixed Wanna with its sparkling
green eyes. Then it turned its head to one side
and opened its jaws.

Wanna
screamed. *Gak!*

The raptor lashed its snout from
side to side, gnashing its jaws together.

'It can't reach us,' Tom realized,
breathing a sigh of relief.

'It's close enough!' Jamie mumbled. The stiff scaly quills of the raptor's feathery crest were brushing across his trainers, and he could see each individual scale on the raptor's snout shimmering like butterfly wings. It smelt of sweaty football boots and musty feather pillows.

With a final frustrated *creech!* the raptor's head disappeared from view. There was a pitter-pattering noise, then everything went quiet.

'We should wait for a while before we check the coast's clear,' Tom whispered.

'We've never seen a raptor *that* big before,' Jamie murmured, quietly extracting the Fossil Finder from his backpack and turning it on. He bent over the screen.

'It's a Utahraptor!' he hissed, reading from the page that popped up. '*THE LARGEST RAPTOR YET FOUND, ONE OF THE DEADLIEST PREDATORS EVER.*'

Tom stepped away from the cave wall and cautiously peered outside. 'And it's right there, waiting for us,' he groaned. 'We can't go back that way.'

Behind them, Nacho was sniffing and scrabbling at a pile of stones.

Woof!

He barked softly, wagging his tail.

'He's found something,' Jamie said.

'Not another dino-rabbit,' Tom groaned.
He threw himself at Nacho and grabbed
him by the collar. 'It's *not* another dino,' he
exclaimed from his position on the ground.
'I can feel air coming in back here.'

Jamie rushed over and started pulling
away the loose stones. There was a
narrow tunnel leading upwards,
with light at the end of it.

'Clever boy!' he told
Nacho. 'You found a secret
escape route.'

They scrambled
up the narrow dark
tunnel and pulled
themselves
out,

blinking in the daylight. They had emerged onto the sandy grass, right by Fang Rock. Wanna and Nacho danced around them in glee.

'Aw, they're happy we're all back together,' Tom said.

'I'm happy we're all in one piece!' said Jamie.

He gave
Wanna and
Nacho a dino and
dog treat to celebrate.
Wanna gulped down his gingko and rubbed
his head lovingly against Nacho, and the little
puppy rolled over and let him gently butt his
tummy, leaving a trail of gingko drool.

'Let's get him back to Agnes before he
causes any more trouble,' said Tom, tickling
Nacho behind the ears. 'Wish we had a lead.'

'Why don't we make one?' Jamie suggested.

He tugged down a straggly creeper that was
dangling from Fang Rock. He stripped off the
leaves and tied it through Nacho's collar.

'Right, Nacho,' Jamie said, taking hold of the end of the lead. 'Now it really, really is time to go home. We've all had plenty of adventure for one trip!'

Tom, Jamie, and Nacho turned to go.

Grunk!

Wanna sat down and refused to budge.

'He wants a collar and lead, too!' Tom laughed. He tugged down a couple more creepers and tied one round Wanna's scaly neck, taking care that it wasn't too tight. Then he tied a creeper lead like Nacho's to Wanna's collar. Wanna trotted proudly beside Tom as they headed across the Plains towards Gingko Hill.

'What's it like, walking a pet dino?' Jamie asked him.

'Awesome!' Tom grinned.

But as Tom spoke, their dino friend froze and glanced wildly around. Tom pulled on the creeper lead, but Wanna dug in his heels.

Jamie and Nacho stopped too. Jamie held his breath. He could hear a rumbling noise, and it was coming closer. The ground began to shake.

'It's the albie again,' he groaned. 'And there's nowhere to hide!'

'Freeze!' Tom cried as the predator thundered towards them, kicking up a cloud of dust. 'Movement catches its attention,' he hissed. 'It might lose interest if we don't move.'

Jamie could feel Nacho and Wanna shaking with fear.

The albertosaurus paused and sniffed at the ground.

'It's still interested,' Tom muttered.

Nacho pulled the lead out of Jamie's hand and raced towards the albie, barking furiously

as he ran rings
round it. But this
time the albie
wasn't distracted.
Its beady eyes were
fixed on Wanna,
Tom, and Jamie
and it strutted towards
them, gnashing its teeth.
Nacho ran back to them and
hid behind Jamie's legs.

Jamie's blood ran
cold. There was no
hiding place and no
sandstorm to save
them now.

The albertosaurus opened
its fearsome jaws. It was
dribbling.

Gurrr!

It roared.

Jamie wondered if it would hurt to be
eaten. He squeezed his eyes shut and waited
for the final chomp.

The ground beneath his feet rumbled.

He didn't feel
the albie's jaws closing
over him —instead, there
was a familiar bellow
from behind.

Aroop!

Jamie swung round.

The ankies were back! They
trooped towards the albertosaurus.
The predator turned and stared

at them as they
surrounded it.
Jamie
glanced at
Tom. He was
grinning
from ear
to ear.
He held
up an imaginary
microphone.
'Right in front of our
eyes,' Tom said in his wildlife

presenter's voice, 'we're witnessing an amazing real-life drama. A hungry albertosaurus has been put off its dinner—that's us, by the way—by a herd of angry ankylosaurs . . .'

Gurrr!

The albie growled, turning its great
head from side to side as the big ankies
moved in like a circle of armoured
tanks.

'This
time, the ankies
are determined to see
off their deadly enemy,' Tom
continued. 'An albertosaurus is no match
for an army that sticks together . . .'

Thwack!

The biggest ankies swiped at
the albertosaurus with their clubs,
making it leap and twist in the
air to avoid them. The albie
charged through a gap
between the ankies
and dashed away
across the plains.

'The mighty
carnivore knows
it's outnumbered,'
Tom announced.
'All it can do is run
away . . . '
'Go, ankies!'
Jamie and Tom
leapt in the air
and gave each
other a high five
as the vicious lizard
disappeared over the
skyline.

Nacho ran up to
a baby anky, wagging
his tail as if he wanted
to make friends.

'Nacho, come back!' Jamie yelled as a big
anky advanced towards him.

Swish.

The anky's tail narrowly missed flattening the puppy.

Nacho's ears dropped and he squatted on the ground as the little anky skittered off with its mother.

'That scared him so much, he's done a poo!' Jamie chuckled.

'You'll have to pick it up,' Tom giggled. 'We can't leave anything here in case it gets fossilized—and that includes puppy poo.'

swish

Jamie sighed and
rummaged in his backpack
for one of the plastic poo
bags Agnes had given
him. Wanna and Nacho
watched with interest as
Jamie reluctantly picked up
the steaming pile. It felt warm and squidgy
through the bag.

'Ugh!' he muttered, tying a knot in the top
of the stinky bag. He wrapped a second bag
around the first and gingerly held it by the
loop at the top.

'Let's get out of here!' He grabbed Nacho's
lead. Tom picked up Wanna's.

Nacho and Wanna sprinted to the river,
Tom and Jamie clinging to the leads as the
puppy and dino pulled them along. The
sandstorm had dumped great piles of sand
into the water, making it easy to cross. Nacho

and Wanna dragged the boys
up Gingko Hill, and they
slithered through the gingko
sludge to the cave. Jamie stood
beside the trail of dinosaur
footprints that seemed to lead
magically out of the rock-face.

'We got back in double-
quick time,' he panted.

Tom nodded. 'Nacho and
Wanna would make a good
team of huskies.' He untied
Wanna's collar and lead.

'It was fun pretending
you were a pet, Wanna,'
he said. 'But now you have
to go back to the wild—
until we meet up next time.'

Wanna wagged his tail
and picked up a fallen gingko

fruit. But instead of gulping it down, he nudged it towards Nacho.

'Awww,' Jamie said, 'he knows it's time to say goodbye.'

Nacho scrunched up his muzzle and took a lick at the stinky fruit.

N . . . n . . . *nacho!* He sneezed. Then he wagged his tail and nudged the fruit back to Wanna. The little dino carefully picked up the gingko and carried it over to his nest of twigs in the corner of Gingko Cave. He gave a deep, contented sigh and curled up in his bed. Nacho trotted over and snuggled up next to him. In an instant, he was fast asleep.

Puppy snores rumbled round the cave on Gingko Hill.

'He's having his afternoon nap at last,' Tom said, removing Nacho's lead and hoisting the exhausted ball of fluff out of Wanna's bed. Wanna looked up, twitched his tail, and closed his eyes.

'Bye, Wanna,' Tom and Jamie whispered.

Then, with Tom carrying the sleeping Nacho and Jamie holding on tight to the bag of poo, they stepped backwards in Wanna's fresh footprints, and flashed back to their secret cave in Dinosaur Cove.

149

CHAPTER 12

Jamie flicked on his torch and shone the light on the poo bag.

'Hope it's turned to dust,' he murmured. But no such luck—it was still fresh and squishy.

Jamie turned the beam of light on Tom and Nacho opened his eyes.

Woof!

He squirmed in Tom's arms, jumped to the floor and trotted to the gap in the secret cave.

'Not again,' groaned Jamie.

'Follow him!' Tom yelled, squeezing
through the gap. He chased Nacho
through Smugglers' Cave and
out into the sunlight on
Smuggler's Point.

The puppy picked his way through the
boulders and bounded down the path towards
the old lighthouse where the Dinosaur

Museum was and Jamie, his dad, and Grandad lived.

A woman with a floppy hat was coming up the path.

'Nacho!' Agnes exclaimed in delight as the puppy hurled itself into her arms and licked her face. 'I was looking for you. Where have you been?'

'He was playing in the caves,' Tom told Agnes. 'We were just on our way back with him.'

'He's had a bit of an adventure,' Jamie added.

Tom glanced at Jamie and raised his eyebrows. Agnes had no idea what sort of adventure!

'No wonder he's tired out now,' Agnes said. She stroked Nacho's silky ears. 'I'll take him home for his nap.'

She spotted the poo bag swinging from Jamie's hand.

'Good to see you cleared up after him,' said Agnes, taking the bag. 'I'll put that in the bin on my way home.'

Agnes set off down the path, Nacho wriggling in her arms. He put his head over Agnes's shoulder.

Woof!

Nacho barked.

Woof woof!

'Bye, Nacho,' Tom and Jamie called.

Jamie looked at Tom. 'Dinosaurs are much less trouble than dogs,' he whispered. 'We never have to pick up dino poo!'

'We'd need to take some really big bags with us if we did!' Tom grinned.

Woof!

DINOSAUR WORLD

- - - - BOYS' ROUTE

Jungle

Misty
Lagoon

White
Ocean

156

Far Away Mountains

Great Plains

Fang Rock

Crashing Rock Falls

Gingko Hill

157

GLOSSARY

Alamosaurus (al-am-oh-sor-us) – a gigantic dinosaur with a vegetarian diet that searched for food with its long neck and tiny head while protecting itself with its long, whip-like tail.

Albertosaurus (albie) (al-bert-oh-sor-us) – a meat-eating dinosaur with a huge tail and two strong legs, but two tiny arms. It was very similar to Tyrannosaurus Rex, but smaller.

Ankylosaurus (ankie) (an-ki-low-sor-us) – a vegetarian dinosaur known for its armoured coat and clubbed tail. Its armour consisted of large bony bumps similar to the covering of modern-day crocodiles and lizards.

Corythosaurus (kor-ith-oh-sor-us) – a duck billed dinosaur that used hundreds of tiny teeth at the back of its beak to crush and grind plants. It had a rounded bony crest at the back of its head.

Cretaceous (cret-ay-shus) – from about 65 to 150 million years ago, this time period was home to the widest variety of dinosaur and insect life of any period. Birds replaced winged dinosaurs, while in the sea, sharks and rays multiplied.

Gingko (gink-oh) – a tree native to China called a 'living fossil' because fossils of it have been found dating back millions of years, yet they are still around today. Also known as the stink bomb tree because of its smelly apricot-like fruit.

Hadrosaurus (had-ro-sor-us) – a type of plant-eating dinosaur. This family includes the Corythosaurus and Lambeosaurus. The fronts of these dinosaurs' heads were flat with duck bills, and they had thousands of teeth in the back of their mouths.

Lambeosaurus (lam-bee-oh-sor-us) – a vegetarian dinosaur with an axe-shaped crest at the back of its head. It had a small beak and a long straight tail.

Old English sheepdog – a large dog with a long, thick, shaggy grey and white coat. It used to be called 'the shepherd's dog' and likes to herd other animals – sometimes even people.

Pterodactyl (ter-oh-dak-til) – a flying prehistoric reptile which could be as small as a bird or as large as an aeroplane.

Sand storm – a storm caused by loose sand and dust being blown around by strong winds. It looks like a giant, solid wall of moving sand.

Triceratops (T-tops) (try-serra-tops) – a three-horned, plant-eating dinosaur which looks like a rhinoceros.

Utahraptor (yoo-tah-rap-tor) – a large meat-eating dinosaur. It was a feathered two-legged dinosaur as tall as a giraffe, and had a snout lined with pointy fangs. It is the largest raptor yet discovered. Named after the place it was discovered: Utah in the USA.

Wannanosaurus (wah-nan-oh-sor-us) – a dinosaur that only ate plants and used its hard, flat skull to defend itself. Named after the place it was discovered: Wannano in China.